THE KING

LIGHTNING McQUEEN

SHERIFF

DOC HUDSON

CHICK

Published by Hachette Partworks Ltd.
ISBN: 978-1-908648-93-8
Date of Printing: June 2016
Printed in Romania by Canale

DISNEY·PIXAR

hachette

Hotshot rookie Lightning McQueen's dream was to win the Piston Cup – and now it was race day! It was a hard race. Current champion the King and rough racer Chick were both determined to win. When everyone else pulled into pit row to change tyres, Lightning kept going. But just a few metres from the finishing line, Lightning's tyres blew, allowing the King and Chick to catch up.

The race was a three-way tie, so there would be a rematch in California. Lightning wanted to get in as much training as possible, so he boarded Mack the trailer and set off right away.

They drove all night. Exhausted, both Lightning and Mack dozed off – and neither of them noticed when Lightning slid off the trailer!

Lightning woke up in a little town called Radiator Springs, to find that he was driving the wrong way, straight into traffic!

In a panic, Lightning knocked over a statue and pulled it along, tearing up the road.

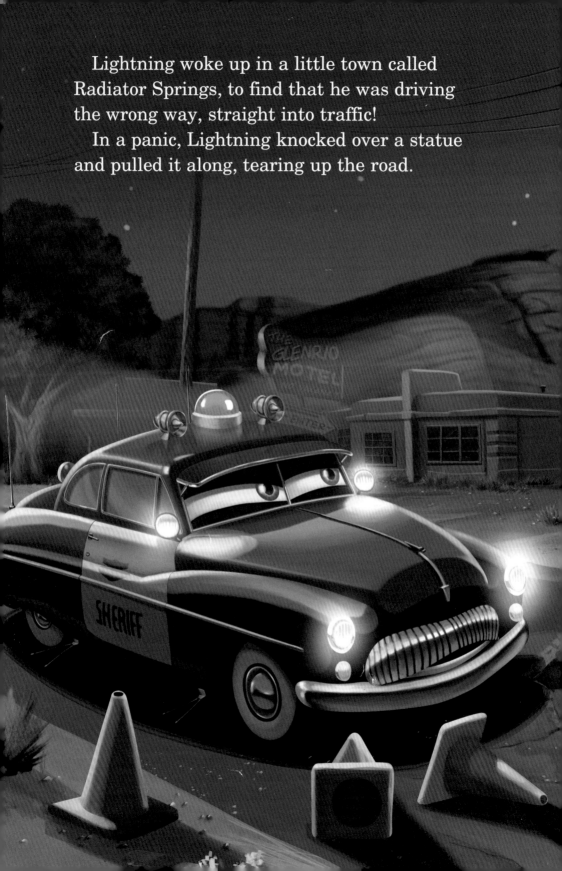

With the town sheriff hot on his trail, Lightning ended up tangled in some power lines. Boy, was he in trouble now!

The next day, a friendly
tow truck called Mater took
him to the courthouse.
Sally the attorney
suggested that Lightning
be made to repair the
road before he could
leave town.

"You'll fix the road under my supervision," ruled
Doc Hudson, the judge.
Lightning did the job as quickly as he could. He
had to make it to California in time for the race!

But when Doc came to inspect Lightning's
work, he wasn't impressed.

"You were supposed to fix
the road, not make it worse,"
he said. "Start over again!"

"But I'm not a bulldozer, I'm a race car," argued Lightning.

"A race car?" said Doc. "Then why don't me and you have a little race?"

"If you win, you can leave. If I win, you do the road my way," said Doc.

Everyone in town hurried to Willy's Butte to watch the race. Lightning roared off, leaving Doc behind in a cloud of dust. But a few minutes later, Lightning missed a turn, skidded off the road and landed right in the middle of a cactus patch. **OUCH!**

So Lightning fixed the road again. He did a good job – the townspeople were impressed.

Lightning went back to Willy's Butte to learn how to make the turn he had missed. Doc told him: turn right to go left. Lightning tried it, but he missed the turn again!

Meanwhile, the new road had inspired everyone in town to smarten up their shops. Lightning decided to visit Doc's garage.

To his amazement, Lightning found three
Piston Cups among all the clutter. Doc used
to be a champion race car! Just then, Doc
appeared. Furious that his secret was
out, he ordered Lightning to go.

Later, Lightning found Doc at Willy's Butte.
"How could you quit at the top of your game?"
Lightning asked.

Doc explained that he had been badly damaged
in a crash; and when he finally returned to the
race circuit, an ambitious rookie – just like
Lightning – had taken his place. Since
then, Doc didn't trust race cars.

The next day, the town was flooded with journalists. They had been searching for Lightning – and now they'd found him!

McQueen knew he had to leave for California. Sadly, he slipped out of town without saying goodbye to anyone.

At last, it was race day! But Lightning was missing his friends in Radiator Springs too much to focus properly on the race ahead.

Then he spotted someone familiar. It was Doc – and he had brought a crew with him, to help Lightning win!

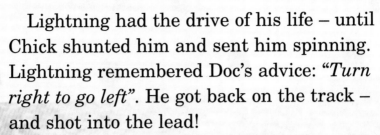

Lightning had the drive of his life – until
Chick shunted him and sent him spinning.
Lightning remembered Doc's advice: *"Turn
right to go left"*. He got back on the track –
and shot into the lead!

Chick was so furious that he rammed the
King, making him crash. Lightning couldn't
let the King end his career as Doc had, so he
went back to help the King finish the race.

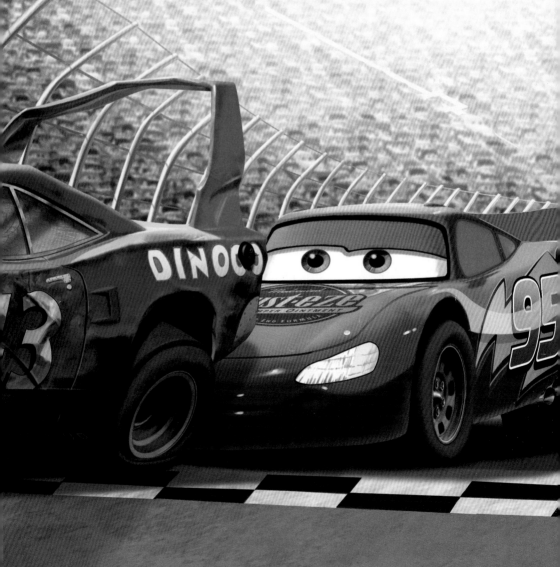

"Woo-hoo! I won!" yelled Chick, but nobody noticed – they were too busy cheering Lightning and the King. Doc was so proud!

Lightning set up a new racing HQ at Radiator Springs. He had found true friends – and from now on, he was going to stick with them!

FILLMORE

GUIDO & LUIGI

MATER

RAMONE

SALLY